SLUGGY FREELANCE

BOOK 4

www.sluggy.com

GAME CALLED ON ACCOUNT OF NAKED CHICK

SLUGGY FREELANCE

www.sluggy.com

Sluggy Freelance: Game Called on Account of Naked Chick is an original publication of Pete Abrams and is published by Plan Nine Publishing, Inc.

Contents © 2000 by Pete Abrams
ISBN 1-929462-09-3
First Printing September 2000

PLAN NINE PUBLISHING

1237 Elon Place
High Point, NC 27263-9745
(336) 454-7766
www.plan9.org

*Bringing you the future tomorrow,
but what's funny today!*

Printed in the USA.

2

Introduction

I still remember the first day I read Sluggy Freelance. A lop-eared bunny rabbit named "Bun-bun" was threatened with neutering, and the cute round li'l fella went tribal on Torg's ass.

Shocking.

Then the sanguine bunny went and torpedoed Torg's chances at a job by calling the employer up and calling his daughter "Mary Lee the Guarantee."

Astonishing.

Then a bit further on, Bun-bun, in his own sweet way, gets Torg smoked by a biker in a bar.

Hysterical. And addicting.

If nothing else, Pete's ability to deviate from expectations – which is not at all the same as not meeting them – is a gift that most artists of any sort wish that they had. Yes, Sluggy has cool art, and the writing is always entertaining, but the way that Pete flawlessly blends both elements together is where he shines.

For the last two years plus, Pete has worked notoriously hard to keep surprising us with his vision, twisted though it may be. After a while though, his way of looking at things starts to seem normal, and the rest of the world is what seems out of touch. What does that say about us? That we're susceptible to the evil machinations of skilled 'toonists like Pete Abrams? I think what it says about Pete is more important: that he's a master of his craft, and we are all but innocents in a world where sociopathic bunnies reign supreme.

Either way, I know we'll all continue to support Pete in what he does. Now that he's a father (congratulations!) he has to display some semblance of normality, but we all know the real truth.

Hats off to you, bud. You done all of us proud.

J.D. "Illiad" Frazer
May 2000

3

Thanks to my wife, Rachel, for her encouragement and patience with this beast named Sluggy. And to my loyal side-kick, "Shirt-Guy" Tom Ricket and his wife Kim for surviving through the mountain that was named "Quatrix Shirts" as well as countless other things. Thanks to my best bud Joe Horton for helping me so much with the coloring of the bonus story. And thanks to Maria (aka tom (s)pawn) for all her help and dedication! Thanks to Bill Holbrook and Illiad for the nice stuff they said about my comic. And apologies to Ian McDonald for Bruno the Bandit's micro-cameo in the bonus story.

Most of all, thanks to the Sluggites! It's because of you (spreading the word about the comic and getting your friends addicted, even though it sometimes requires threats of physical violence) that I am where I am today! From what we can tell, thanks to you, Sluggy Freelance seems to spread quickly into an area and take it over. Be it a department at some Ivy League College, or a Tech Support Staff at some major computer retailer, time and time again, the story is the same. Like a hideous virus, it sweeps through and claims all. And like Steven King's The Stand, only 1% of the population is able to resist the virus. It is a good virus that I have made, a funny, addictive virus. But without you, the carriers of the virus, how will my comic ever reach Plague Status? So my thanks to you, the virus carriers of e-ville!!! Go forth and infect! Infect!! INFECT!!! And if you've never heard of Sluggy Freelance and are looking at this comic for the first time, please disregard the last paragraph; you'll like my strip! It's like Ziggy!

4

for Leah

NAME: TORG
DESC.: FREELANCE WEB DESIGNER.

SITUATION: TEST DROVE RIFF'S TIME MACHINE TO THE **YEAR 2000**. THE TIME MACHINE WAS NOT **"Y2K COMPATIBLE"**.
CURRENT CONDITION: TRAPPED IN THE PAST.
SCREWED!

NAME: ZOË
DESC.: COED. COMMUNI-CATIONS MAJOR.

SITUATION: TEST DROVE RIFF'S TIME MACHINE TO THE **YEAR 2000**. THE TIME MACHINE WAS NOT **"Y2K COMPATIBLE"**.
CURRENT CONDITION: TRAPPED IN THE PAST.
SCREWED!

NAME: RIFF
DESC.: FREELANCE BUM, INVENTOR.

SITUATION: ACCIDENTALLY TRAPPED HIS FRIENDS SOMEWHERE IN TIME, NO IDEA HOW TO BRING THEM BACK.
CURRENT CONDITION: UNKNOWN, PRESUMED DEAD.

NAME: BUN-BUN
DESC.: OFFICIAL CUTE TALKING ANIMAL

SITUATION: BLOWN UP WHILE TRYING TO KILL SANTA CLAUS.
CURRENT CONDITION: UNKNOWN, PRESUMED DEAD.

NAME: AYLEE
DESC.: ALIEN FROM ANOTHER DIMENSION/ SECRETARY

SITUATION: FROZEN IN TIME AND SOLD AS A STATUE.
CURRENT CONDITION:
UNKNOWN.

NAME: GWYNN
DESC.: FRIEND OF ZOË, PREVIOUS RELATIONSHIP WITH RIFF.

SITUATION: POSSESSED BY THE DEMON K'Z'K. HER SOUL WAS TAKEN WHEN THE DEMON WAS EXORCISED AND SENT TO THE PAST.
CURRENT CONDITION: SOULLESS VEGETABLE.
COMATOSE.

ALL BUMMED OUT.

NAME: K'Z'K
(KIZKE)
DESC.: DEMON. "THE SOUL COLLECTOR".

SITUATION: UNLEASHED ON THE EARTH BUT BLASTED INTO THE PAST BY TORG AND RIFF. WOULD HAVE CONQUERED THE FUTURE, MAY STILL CONQUER THE PAST.
CURRENT CONDITION: FREE.

NAME: KIKI
DESC.: RIFF'S PET FERRET.
EASILY DISTRAC...

SITUATION: CURRENTLY POINGING AROUND RIFF'S LAB AND... *OOOOH! WHAT'S THIS? OOOOH! WHAT'S THAT?*
CURRENT CONDITION:
ooooOOH!

8

9

10

11

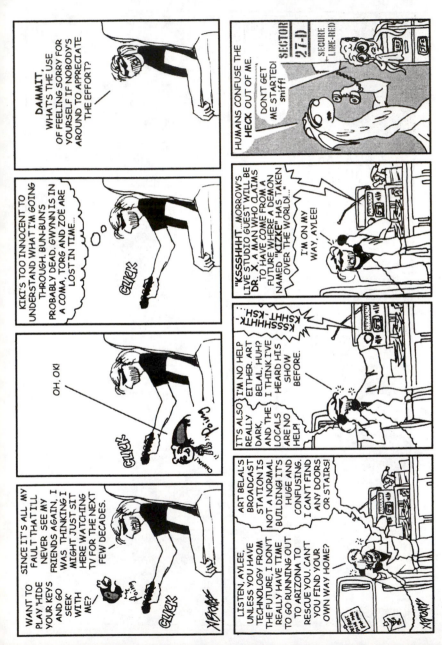

WANT TO PLAY "HIDE YOUR KEYS AND GO SEEK" WITH ME?

SINCE IT'S ALL MY FAULT THAT I'LL NEVER SEE MY FRIENDS AGAIN, I WAS THINKING I MIGHT JUST SIT HERE WATCHING TV FOR THE NEXT FEW DECADES.

CLICK

OH, OK!

CLICK

KIKI'S TOO INNOCENT TO UNDERSTAND WHAT I'M GOING THROUGH. BUN-BUN'S PROBABLY DEAD. GWYNN IS IN A COMA, TORG AND ZOË ARE LOST IN TIME...

CLICK

DAMMIT, WHAT'S THE USE OF FEELING SORRY FOR YOURSELF IF NOBODY'S AROUND TO APPRECIATE THE EFFORT?

LISTEN, AYLEE, UNLESS YOU HAVE TECHNOLOGY FROM THE FUTURE, I DON'T REALLY HAVE TIME TO GO RUNNING OUT TO ARIZONA TO RESCUE YOU. CAN'T YOU FIND YOUR OWN WAY HOME?

ART BELAL'S BROADCAST STATION IS NOT A NORMAL BUILDING! IT'S HUGE AND CONFUSING. I CAN'T FIND ANY DOORS OR STAIRS!

IT'S ALSO REALLY DARK, AND THE LOCALS ARE NO HELP!

I'M NO HELP EITHER, ART BELAL. I THINK I'VE HEARD HIS SHOW BEFORE.

KSSSSHHHTK-KSHT... KSH-

"KSSSHHHT...MORROW'S LIVE STUDIO GUEST WILL BE DR. X, A MAN WHO CLAIMS TO HAVE COME FROM A FUTURE WHERE A DEMON NAMED "CIZKE" HAS TAKEN OVER THE WORLD..."

I'M ON MY WAY, AYLEE!

HUMANS CONFUSE THE **HECK** OUT OF ME.

DON'T GET ME STARTED! sniff!

SECTOR 27-D

SECURE LINE-RED

13

14

16

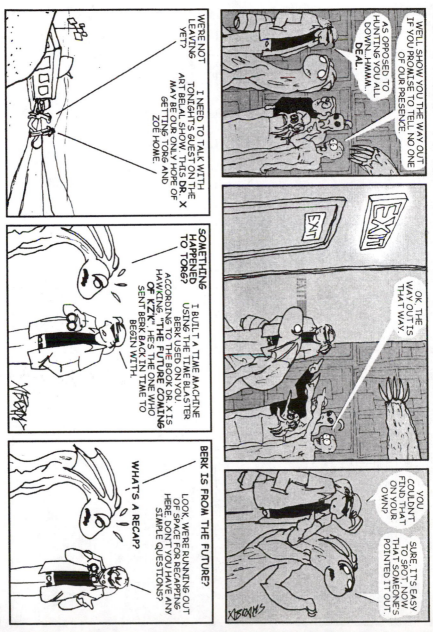

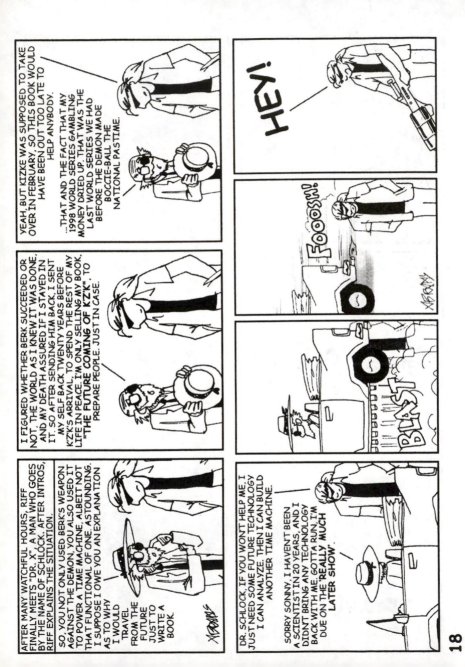

18

19

22

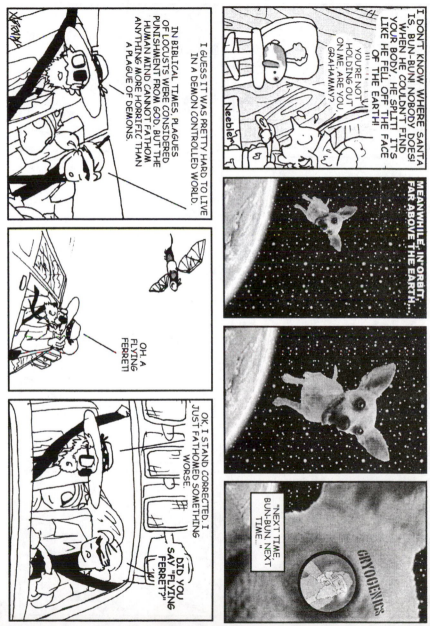

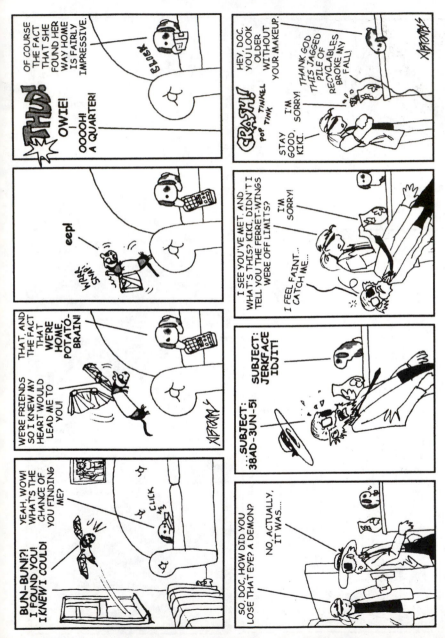

24

DAY 1 OF BUN-BUN TESTING
11-5-97, DR. SCHLOCK ACTING. SUBJECT: 38AD-3UN-5. TODAY I WILL BE TESTING THE EFFECTS OF FORMULA 3Y35 MASCARA AND EYELINER. DUE TO ITS SLIGHTLY RADIOACTIVE NATURE, IT MAY KILL THE SPECIMEN.
MEANWHILE, I'LL BE TESTING THE ACCURACY OF THE REDLIGHT-SIGHT ON MY GLOCK.
BUN-BUN, WHAT HAPPENED BETWEEN US WAS A LONG TIME AGO, LONGER FOR ME THAN YOU I SUPPOSE. LET'S START OVER, SHALL WE?
SURE, PALLY! PUT IT THERE!
POW
CRASH!
WHAM
BAM!
1997
Sluggy Freelance

BUN-BUN, WE NEED DR. SCHLOCK. PLEASE LET HIM OUT OF THE CAGE.
CAN'T. I'VE GOT A LOT MORE EXPERIMENTS THAT NEED A LAB-RAT.
COULD I HAVE SOME MORE NUTRIENT ENRICHED ALFALFA PELLETS PLEASE?
RIFF NEEDS DR. SCHLOCK'S HELP TO RESCUE TORG AND ZOË! YOU HAVE TO LET HIM OUT!
I'M IN A BAD MOOD, ZUCCHINI-FACE! IF YOU WANT TO GO AGAIN, BRING IT ON!
KA-CLICK
BUN-BUN? IS THAT A COMB?
THAT'S IT! YOU'RE ALL ON MY $#!& LIST! I'M OUTTA HERE.
Poing

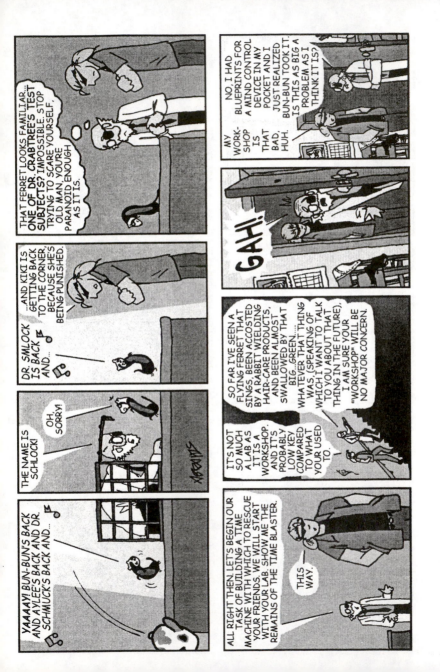

26

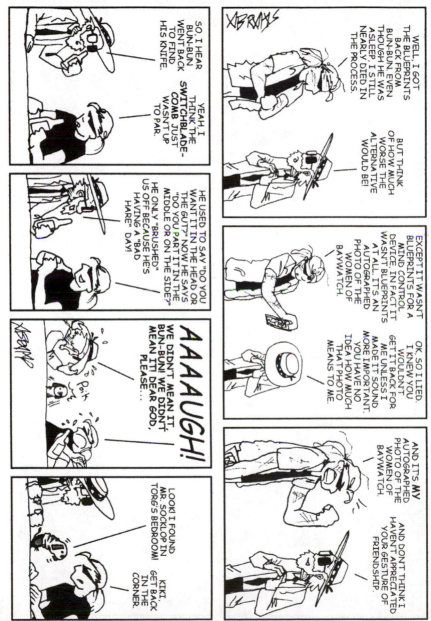

28

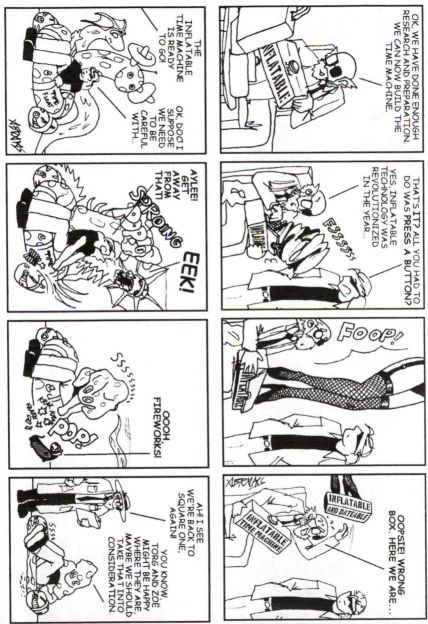

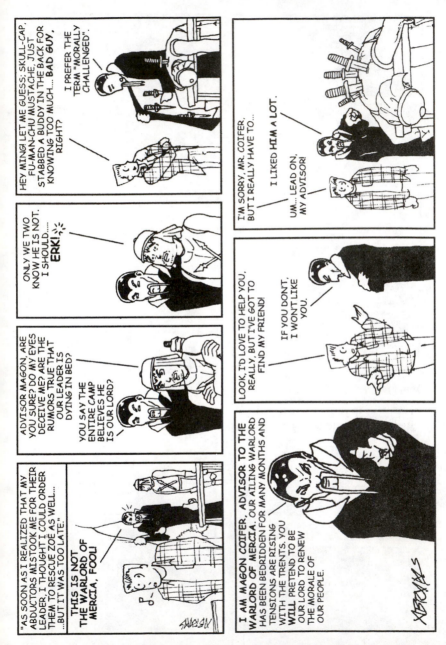

32

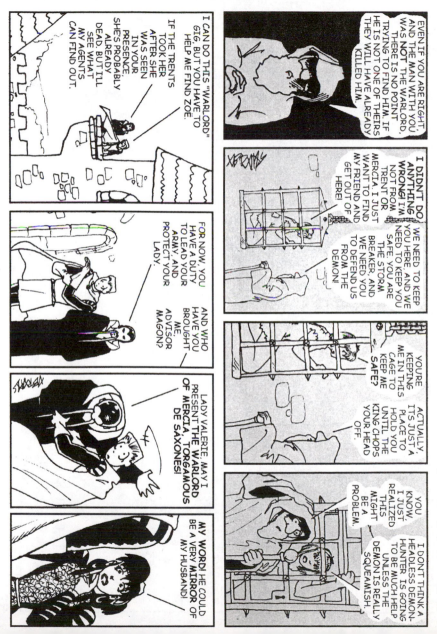

33

34

36

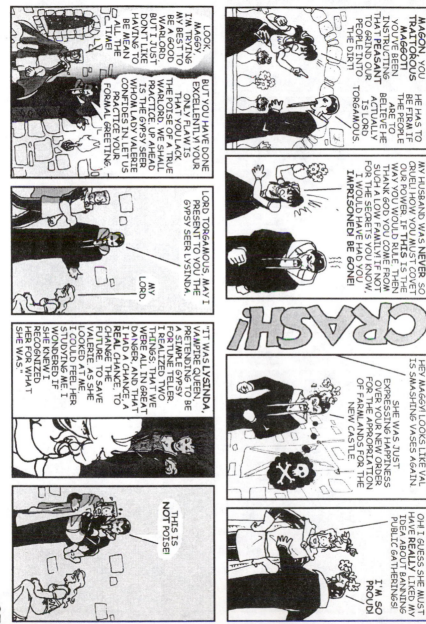

38

40

41

42

I KNOW THE PEOPLE THINK I'M THE WARLORD OF MERCIA, AND YOU WANT ME TO PUBLICLY DECLARE WAR ON THE TRENTS, BUT I CAN'T. I KNOW YOU GUYS THINK WAR IS NO BIG DEAL, BUT IT WILL MEAN THE DEATH OF HUNDREDS OF PEOPLE.

PEOPLE WHO HAD NOTHING TO DO WITH ZOE'S DEATH OR STEALING THE BOOK. IF THAT TRENTS STARTED IT, THEY WOULD BE DIFFERENT. BUT I WON'T BE RESPONSIBLE FOR STARTING A WAR, I CAN'T HAVE THAT ON MY CONSCIENCE.

SO NOW WHAT DO WE DO?

DON'T WORRY, I'VE SENT A LETTER.

MY KING, TORGAMOUS... MUSTACHE SMELL LIKE PARMESAN."

...THIS MEANS WAR!

WE SEARCHED THE LIBRARY FOR MANY DAYS AND NOW WE HAVE FOUND IT! WE HAVE THE BOOK OF E-VILLE!

YOU SHOULD SEE OUR CHILD CARE CENTER!

THIS PLACE IS SO STUPID IT MAKES ME WANT TO RUN SCREAMING AT THE TOP OF MY LUNGS! THAT WASN'T A LIBRARY! IT WAS JUST A HUGE PIT YOU THREW ALL YOUR BOOKS IN!

BEHOLD, KING SIGHARD!

AHHH! I SEE YOU HAVE FOUND THE BOOK. WITH THIS BOOK AND THE STORM BREAKER AT MY SIDE, NOBODY COULD DEFEAT OUR ARMY! WE MARCH TO DESTROY MERCIA IN THE MORNING.

WE'VE GONE TO WAR? WHY?

THEY MADE FUN OF MY MUSTACHE-ODOR.

YEAAAAAA

WHAT SPEED! THE STORM BREAKER HAS. SHE'LL MAKE A FINE ADDITION TO MY ARMY!

DID YOU JUST SAY SOMETHING, MY KING?

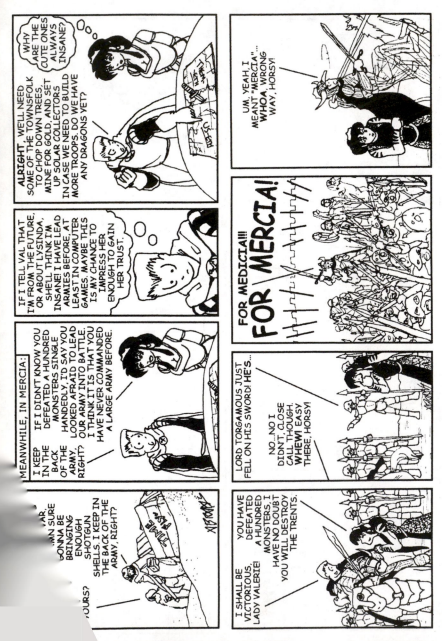

44

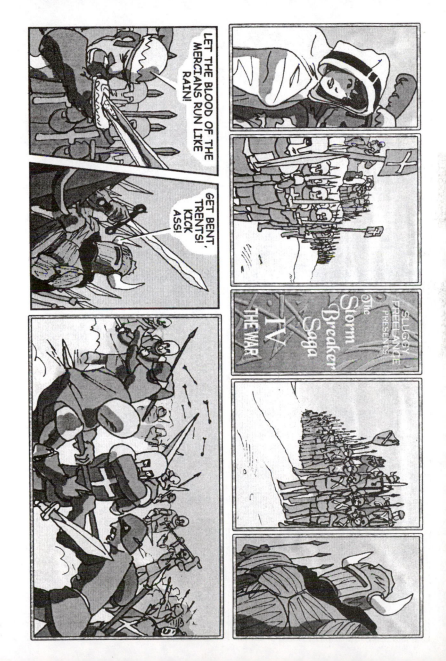

46

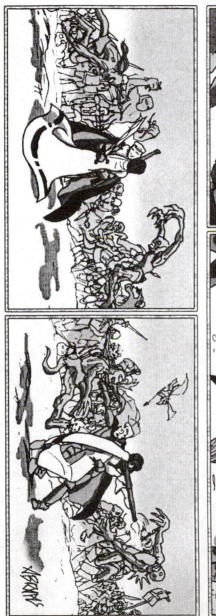

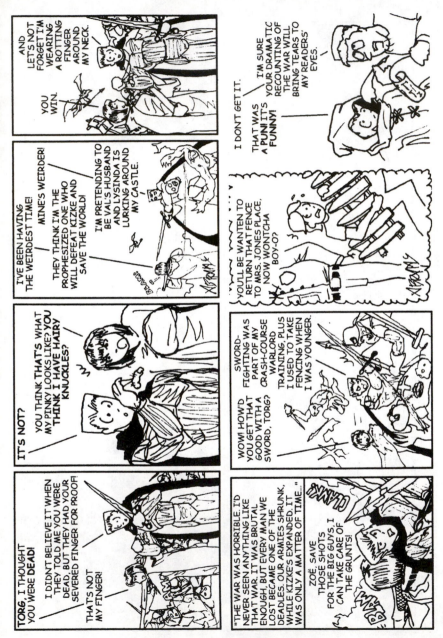

48

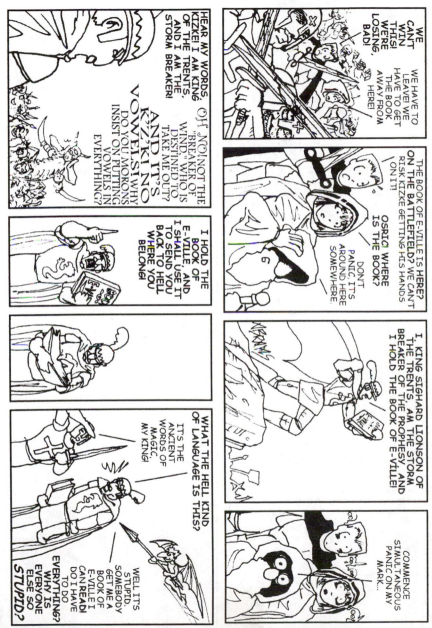

49

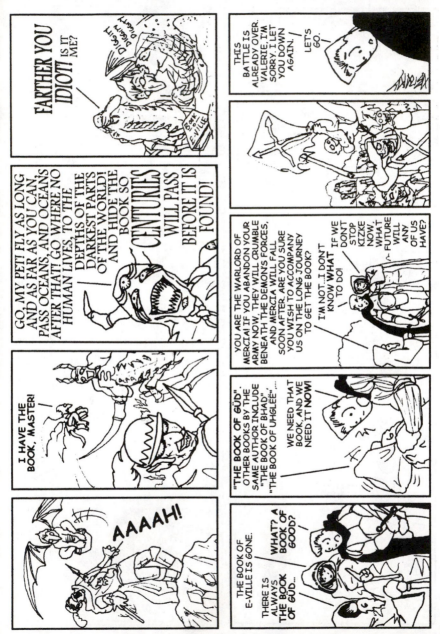

52

54

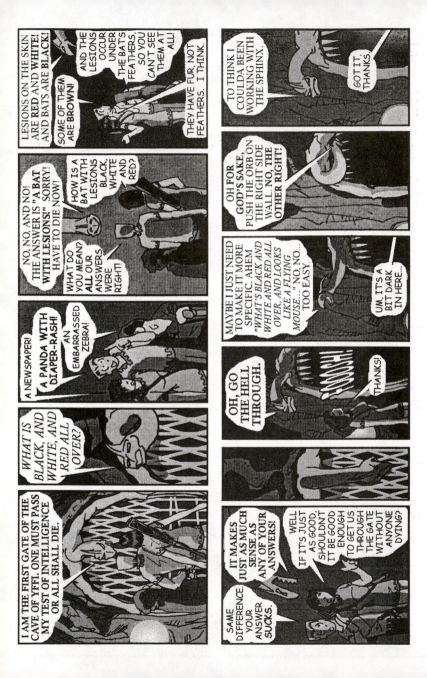

56

57

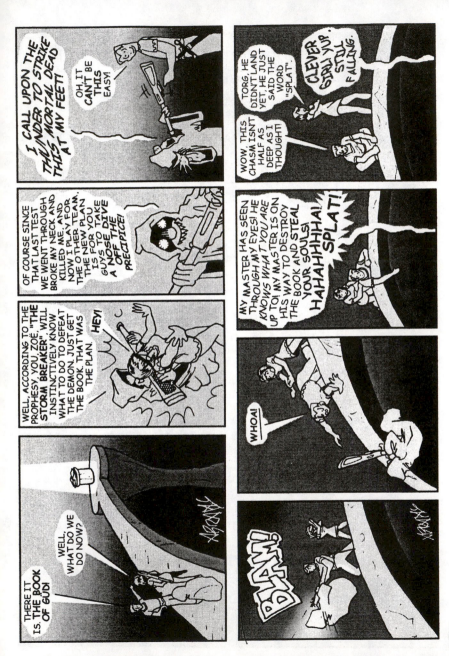

58

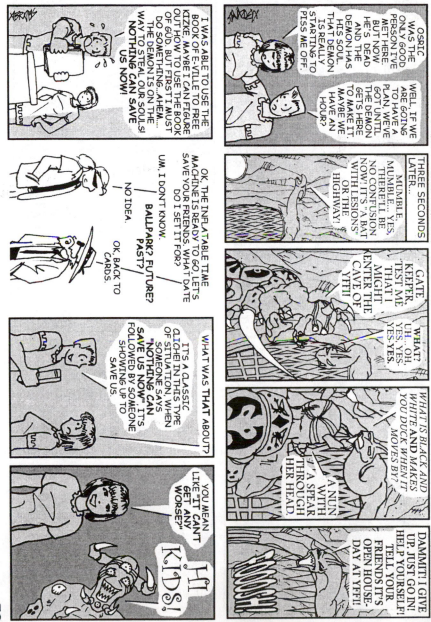

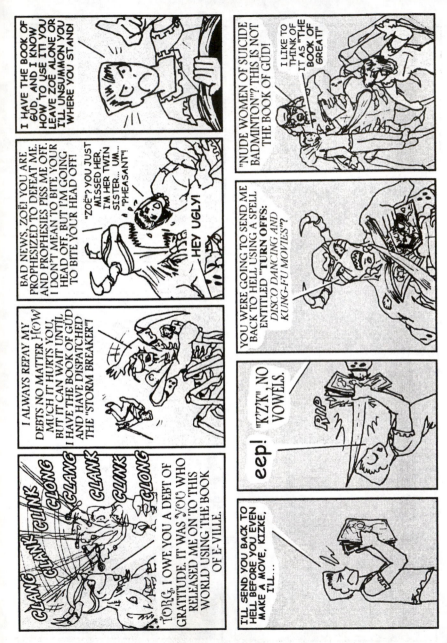

60

61

62

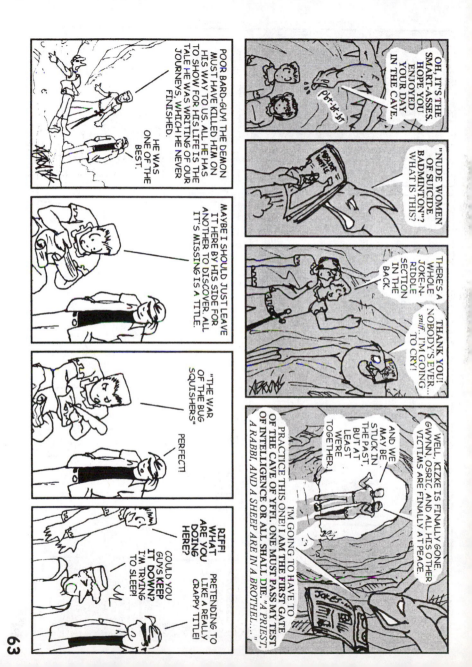

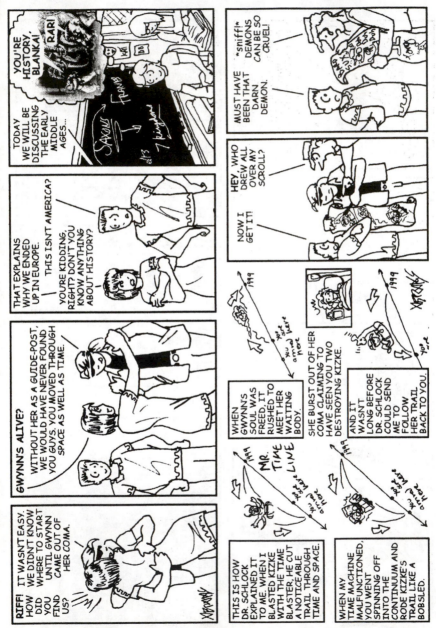

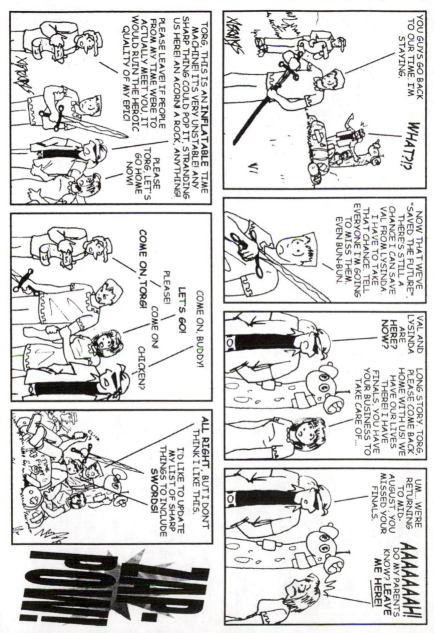

65

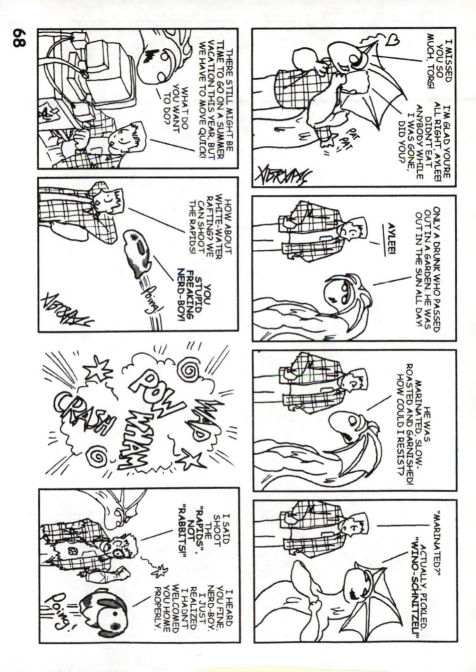

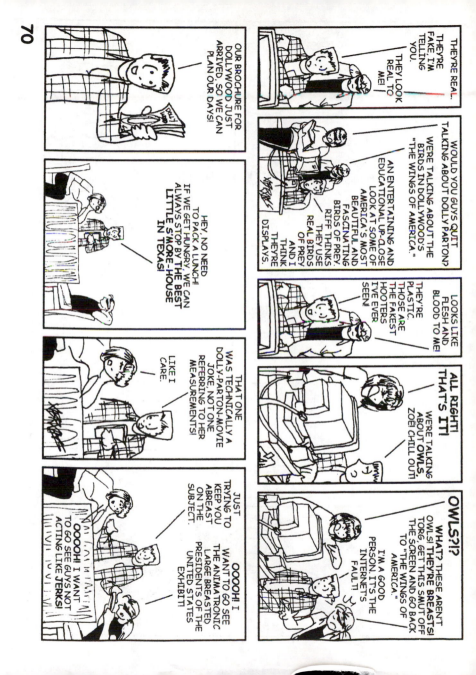

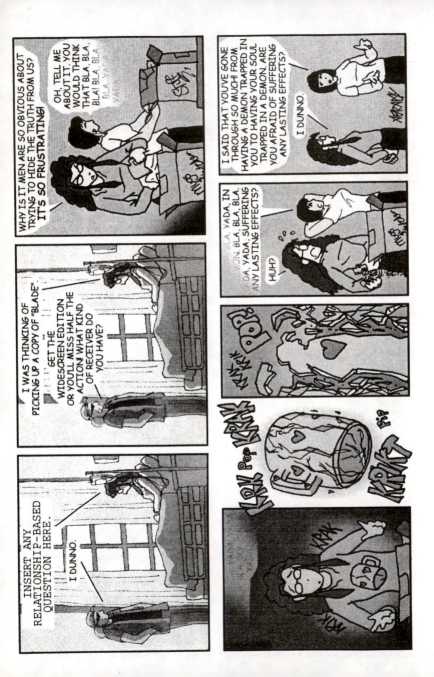

72

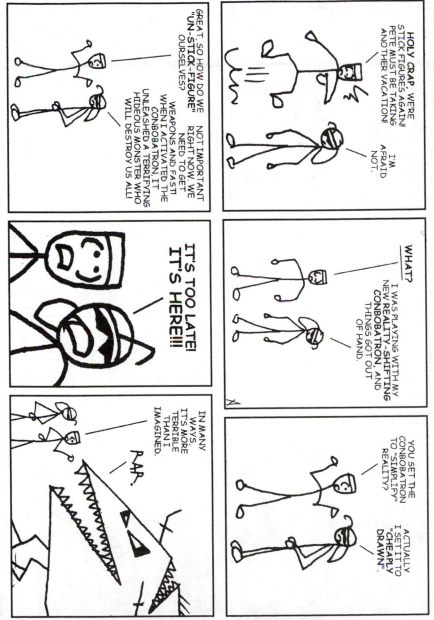

73

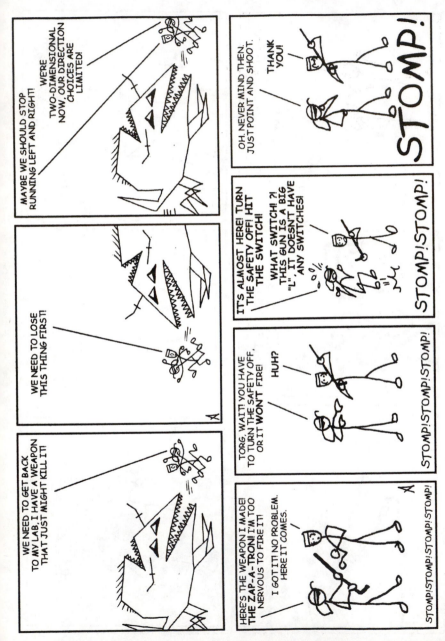

75

SLUGGY
FREELANCE:
STICK
FIGURE

"It looks like
Stick Figure
Week, but is it
more than
what it
seems?"

WEEK
SUNDAY!

76

77

AND ME! KIKI? WHAT ARE YOU DOING HERE?

KIKI, I CAN HONESTLY SAY I'VE NEVER BEEN SO HAPPY TO SEE YOU IN MY ENTIRE LIFE.

NOW THAT IS YOUR STYLE.

VROOOM

THINK OF IT, BUN-BUN. JUST YOU AND ME ON A TWO WEEK ROAD TRIP TO SEE AMERICA! JUST US GUYS, YOU AND ME, A MAN AND HIS RABBIT. THINK OF THE HOURS AND HOURS WE HAVE TO BOND! NOTHING BUT YOU AND ME, BUDDY!

PUNCH IT, KIKI.

BOOT!

ON AN EMPTY WINDING DIRT ROAD IN THE MIDDLE OF NOWHERE...

SO, NOBODY WANTED TO GO ON VACATION WITH ME, HUH? WELL, I DON'T CARE IF NOBODY ELSE WANTS TO COME. I DON'T CARE IF SUMMER IS OVER. NOTHING CAN STOP ME FROM DOING A ROAD TRIP.

DON'T TELL ME YOU INVITED KIKI ALONG TO SHARE OUR VACATION, BUN-BUN. THAT'S NOT YOUR STYLE.

ACTUALLY, NERD-BOY, SHE'S HERE TO WORK THE GAS PEDAL WHEN I STEAL YOUR CAR AND LEAVE YOU BY THE SIDE OF THE ROAD.

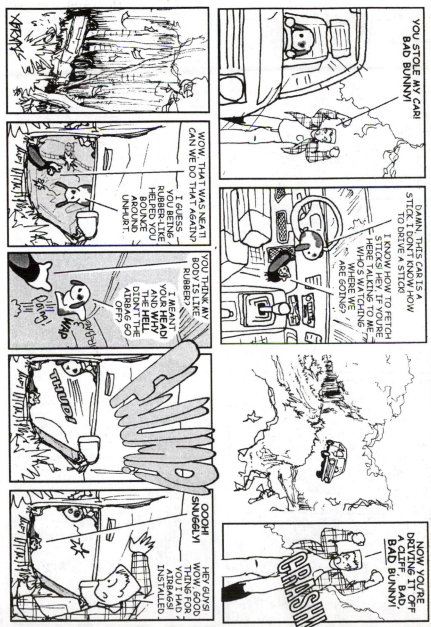

80

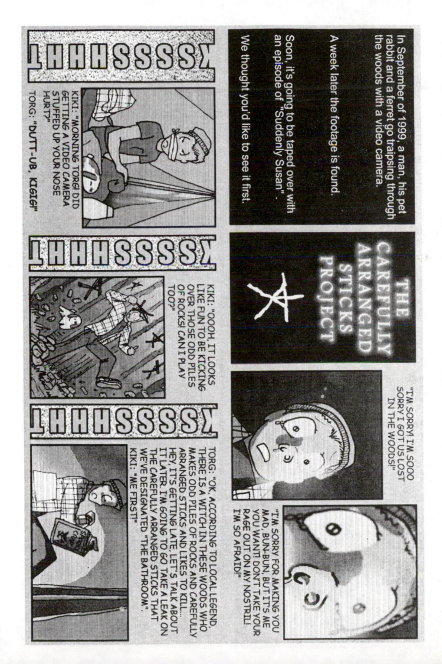

In September of 1999, a man, his pet rabbit and a ferret go traipsing through the woods with a video camera.

A week later the footage is found.

Soon, it's going to be taped over with an episode of "Suddenly Susan".

We thought you'd like to see it first.

THE CAREFULLY ARRANGED STICKS PROJECT

"I'M SORRY! I'M SOOO SORRY I GOT US LOST IN THE WOODS!"

"I'M SORRY FOR MAKING YOU MAD, BUN-BUN, BUT IT'S ME YOU WANT! DON'T TAKE YOUR RAGE OUT ON MY NOSTRIL! I'M SO AFRAID!"

KIKI: "MORNING TORG! DID GETTING A VIDEO CAMERA STUFFED UP YOUR NOSE HURT?"

TORG: "DUTT-UB, KEKI!"

KIKI: "OOOH, IT LOOKS LIKE FUN TO BE KICKING OVER THOSE ODD PILES OF ROCKS! CAN I PLAY TOO?"

TORG: "OK. ACCORDING TO LOCAL LEGEND, THERE IS A WITCH IN THESE WOODS WHO MAKES ODD PILES OF ROCKS AND CAREFULLY ARRANGED STICKS AND LIKES TO KILL... HEY, IT'S GETTING LATE. LET'S TALK ABOUT IT LATER. I'M GOING TO GO TAKE A LEAK ON THE CAREFULLY ARRANGED STICKS THAT WE'VE DESIGNATED "THE BATHROOM.""

KIKI: "ME FIRST!"

82

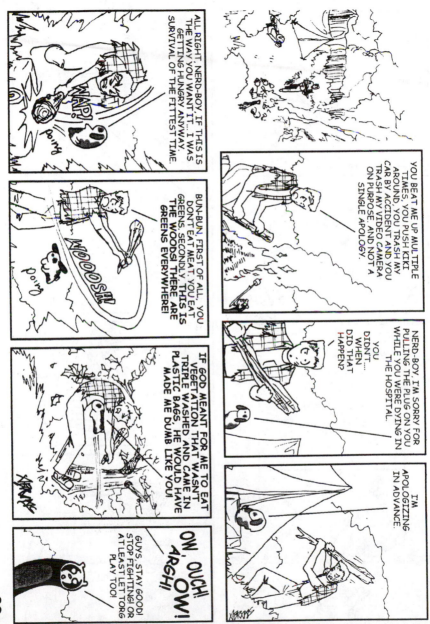

84

SLUGGY FREELANCE

86

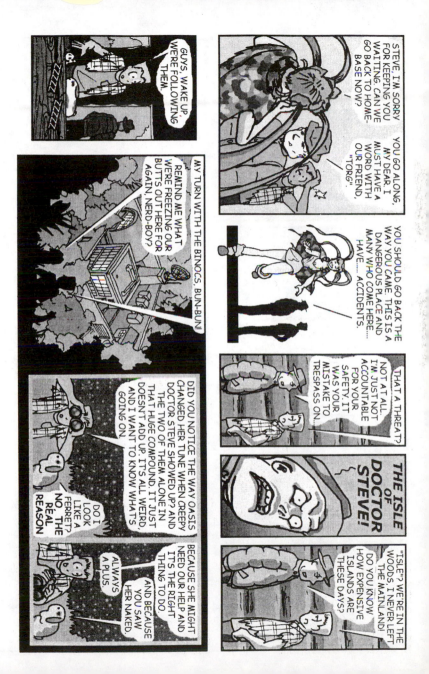

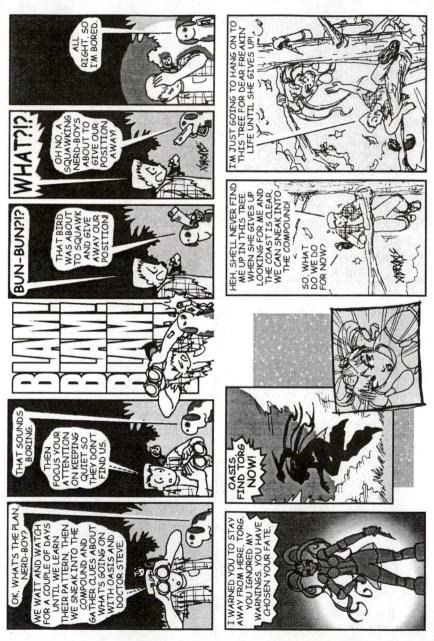

ALL RIGHT, SO I'M BORED.

OH NO, A SQUAWKING NERD-BOY'S ABOUT TO GIVE OUR POSITION AWAY!

WHAT?!?

THAT BIRD WAS ABOUT TO SQUAWK AND GIVE AWAY OUR POSITION!

BUN-BUN?!?

BLAM! BLAM! BLAM! BLAM!

THAT SOUNDS BORING.

THEN FOCUS YOUR ATTENTION ON KEEPING QUIET SO THEY DON'T FIND US.

OK, WHAT'S THE PLAN, NERD-BOY?

WE WAIT AND WATCH FOR A COUPLE OF DAYS UNTIL WE LEARN THEIR PATTERN, THEN WE SNEAK INTO THE COMPOUND AND GATHER CLUES ABOUT WHAT'S GOING ON WITH OASIS AND DOCTOR STEVE.

I'M JUST GOING TO HANG ON TO THIS TREE FOR DEAR FREAKIN' LIFE UNTIL SHE GIVES UP!

HEH, SHE'LL NEVER FIND ME UP IN THIS TREE. WHEN SHE GIVES UP LOOKING FOR ME AND THE COAST IS CLEAR, WE CAN SNEAK INTO THE COMPOUND!

SO, WHAT DO WE DO FOR NOW?

OASIS FIND TORG NOW!

I WARNED YOU TO STAY AWAY FROM HERE, TORG. YOU IGNORED MY WARNINGS. YOU HAVE CHOSEN YOUR FATE.

88

90

TORG, I FOUND YOU! BUN-BUN DIDN'T THINK I COULD!

HOW AM I GOING TO GET YOU OUT OF HERE?

YOU CAN'T, BUT THERE'S A WAY YOU CAN HELP. DOCTOR STEVE HAS OASIS HYPNOTIZED OR BRAINWASHED OR SOMETHING. THE KEY IS HIS WATCH. WHEN HE TALKS INTO HIS WATCH, SHE OBEYS. SO GO GET IT AND BRING IT TO ME!

MOVE QUICKLY, KIKI! DOCTOR STEVE SEEMS A BIT UNSTABLE. I DON'T KNOW HOW LONG I HAVE LEFT.

AND THAT'S "WATCH", NOT "CROTCH"! DON'T SCREW IT UP THIS TIME!

THAT WAS ONE EMBARASSING MAGIC SHOW, I CAN TELL YOU!

OASIS, ON MY MARK, EXECUTE ACTION F-2.

NOW!

GRASNAP!

92

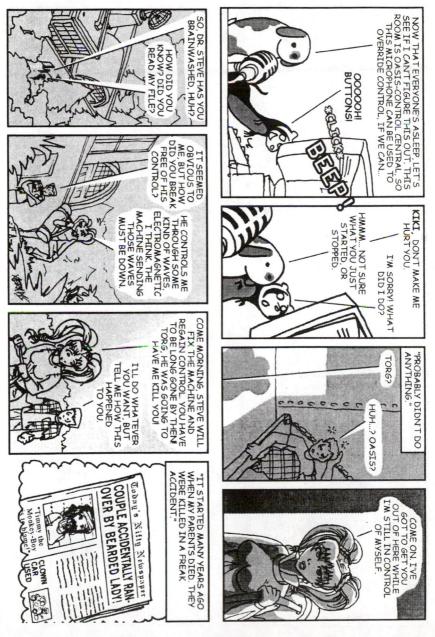

NOW THAT EVERYONE'S ASLEEP, LET'S SEE IF I CAN'T FIGURE THIS OUT. THIS ROOM IS OASIS-CONTROL CENTRAL, SO THIS MICROPHONE CAN BE USED TO OVERRIDE CONTROL, IF WE CAN...

OOOOOH! BUTTONS!

CLICK

BEEP!

KIKI, DON'T MAKE ME HURT YOU.

I'M SORRY! WHAT DID I DO?

HMMM... NOT SURE WHAT YOU JUST STARTED, OR STOPPED.

"PROBABLY DIDN'T DO ANYTHING."

TORG?

HUH..? OASIS?

COME ON I'VE GOT TO GET YOU OUT OF HERE WHILE I'M STILL IN CONTROL OF MYSELF.

SO, DR. STEVE HAS YOU BRAINWASHED, HUH?

HOW DID YOU KNOW? DID YOU READ MY FILE?

IT SEEMED OBVIOUS TO ME. BUT HOW DID YOU BREAK FREE OF HIS CONTROL?

HE CONTROLS ME THROUGH SOME KIND OF WAVES, ELECTROMAGNETIC I THINK. THE MACHINE SENDING THOSE WAVES MUST BE DOWN.

COME MORNING, STEVE WILL FIX THE MACHINE AND REGAIN CONTROL. YOU HAVE TO BE LONG GONE BY THEN TORG, HE WAS GOING TO HAVE ME KILL YOU!

I'LL DO WHATEVER YOU WANT, BUT TELL ME HOW THIS HAPPENED TO YOU.

"IT STARTED MANY YEARS AGO WHEN MY PARENTS DIED. THEY WERE KILLED IN A FREAK ACCIDENT."

Today's Nifty Newspaper

COUPLE ACCIDENTALLY RAN-OVER BY BEARDED LADY!

"Timmy the Monkey-Boy" is back!

CLOWN CAR USED

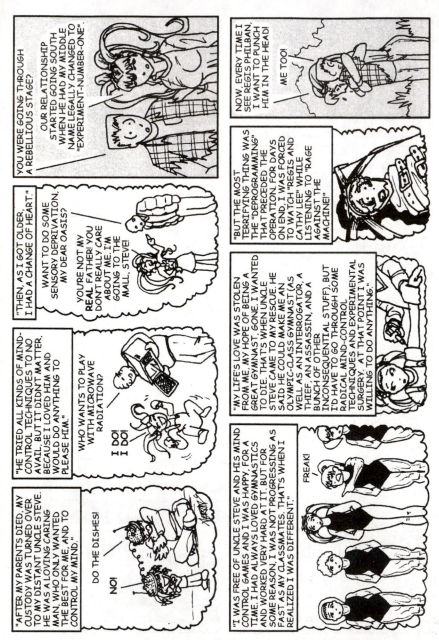

94

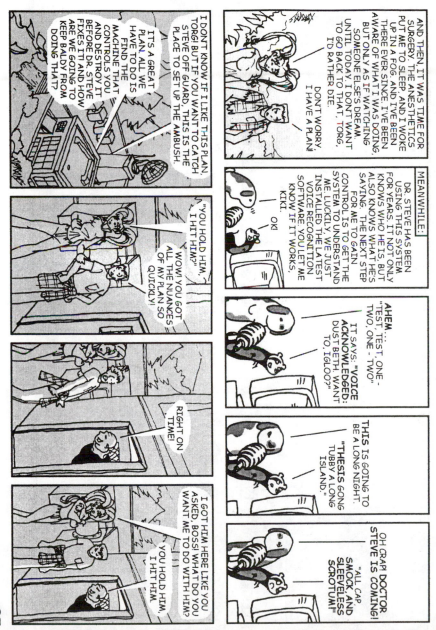

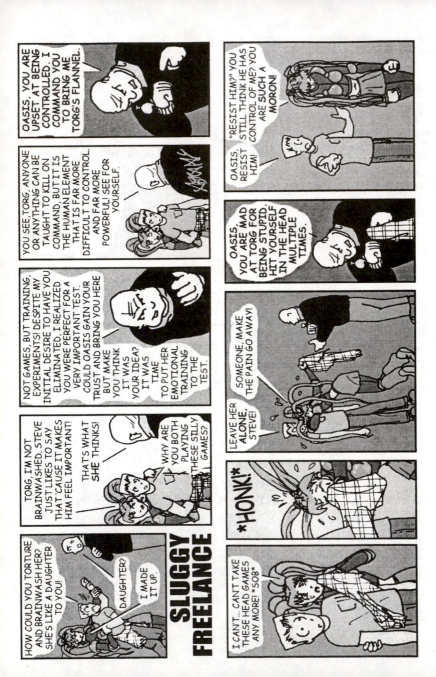

97

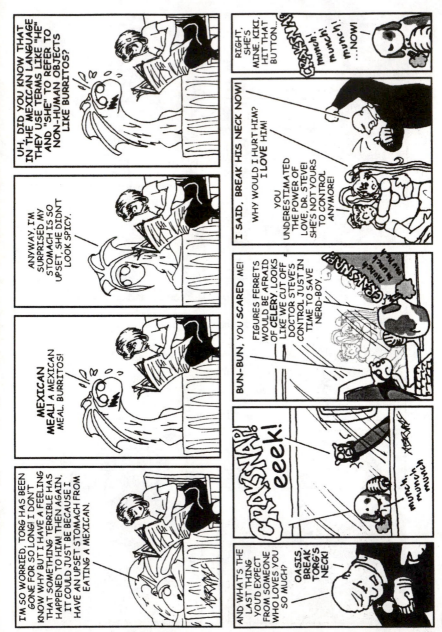

98

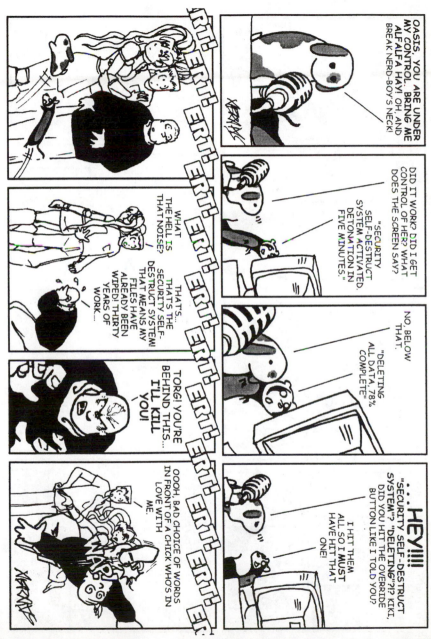

69

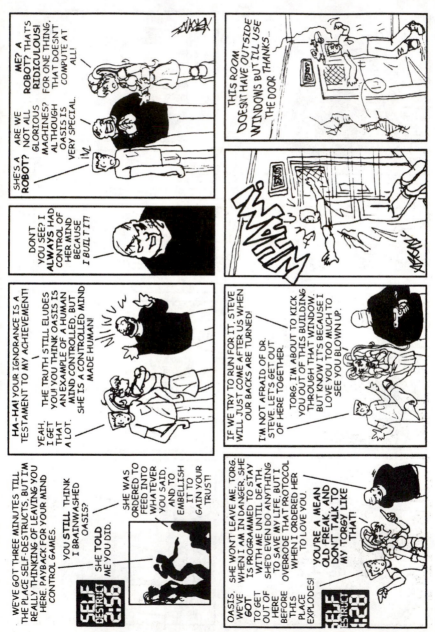

100

SELF DESTRUCT 0:32
DIE!
BLAM!
BLAM!
BLAM!
EXIT
P-TING
P-TANG
GAK!
FFFF
FOOM!
IS EVERYBODY ALL RIGHT?
CAN I HAVE A MARSHMALLOW?
HEY LOOK WHAT I SNAGGED OUT OF STEVEY-BOY'S DESK!
CAR KEYS?
WHOA!
OOOOH, SHINY!

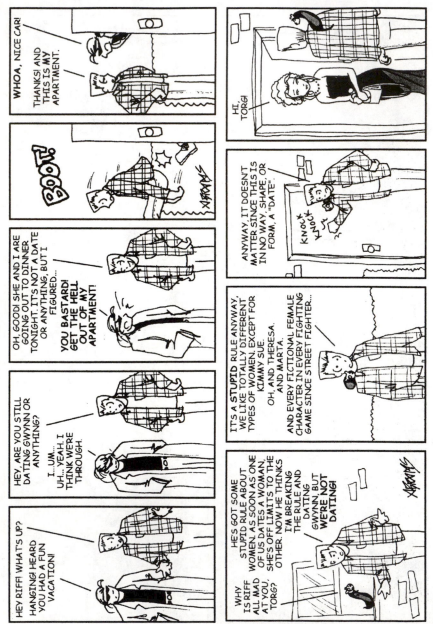

104

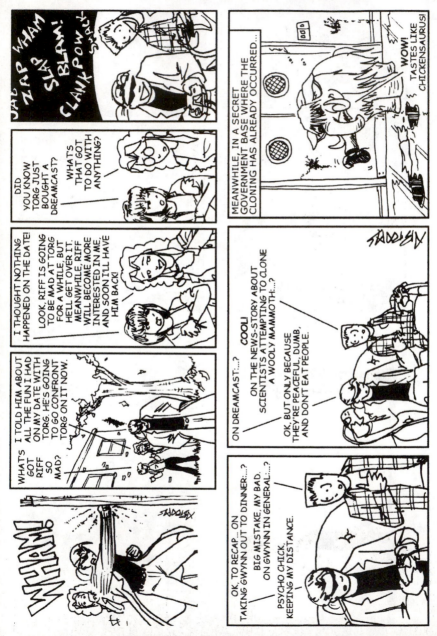

108

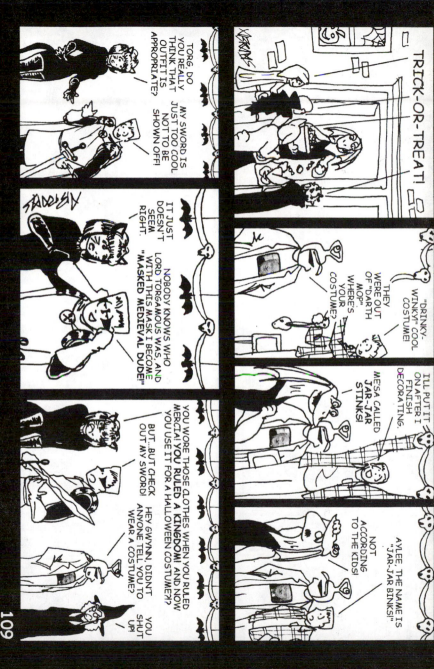

"MY NAME IS GWYNN. A LONG TIME AGO I WAS TAKEN AND POSSESSED BY A DEMON. IT CAUSED ME TO LOSE MY LOVE, MY JOB, MY LIFE."

I DON'T KNOW HOW TO DO A REAL SEANCE ANYWAY.

THEN LET'S DO A FAKE ONE LIKE IN THE MOVIES.

"WHEN I WAS FREED, SOME AMOUNT OF THE DEMONIC POWER I HAD REMAINED. I HIDE FROM IT BUT IT ALLOWS ME TO SENSE THINGS."

OH, THE ONES WHICH **ALWAYS** CAUSE POSSESSION, TERROR, AND DEATH?

YEAH BUT THE TORMENT ONLY LASTS ABOUT AN HOUR AND A HALF.

"FOR SOME REASON, TONIGHT I CAN ALMOST HEAR THE FOOTSTEPS, AND IT SCARES ME."

OH, SPIRITS, HEAR US! BLA, BLA, BLA.

"I TRIED TO WARN THEM, NOT TO DO ANYTHING TO ATTRACT ATTENTION, BUT I HEAR IT WALKING THIS WAY."

"IT'S RUNNING THIS WAY!"

"I HAD NEVER MET HER, BUT I KNEW HER FROM THE STORIES RIFF AND ZOË TOLD ME."

"AND FROM THE WAY SHE LOOKED AT THE CROWD AND SAW ONLY TORG WITH EMPTY EYES."

"THE ONE WHO LOVED TORG MOST, AND WHO DIED BY HIS HAND."

"VAL."

Die for me, love.

12

DIE YOU DEAD UNDEAD GHOST-BEAST!

ZAP ZAP ZAP ZAP

RIFF, YOU CAN'T KILL A GHOST WITH LASERS!

I RECALIBRATED THE LASER TO AFFECT GAMMA-GOZER-WAVES MAKING ECTOPLASM VULNERABLE.

ZAPPO!

WELL, I WOULD HAVE IF I KNEW SHE WAS COMING.

AND WHEN, EXACTLY, DID YOU DO THAT?

ZAP ZAP ZAP ZAP

GUYS! RIFF! WE'RE ON THE OTHER SIDE OF THE GHOST! QUIT SHOOTING!

UM..... HI, VAL!

I am cast into hell.

WHOA! SORRY TO HEAR IT!

I traveled a good life yet can cast into hell. For cripes not in the bit in death. Unfair.

YUP! WELL! UM.... SO! WHAT BRINGS YOU HERE?

Only your love can save me. And until you do—

None shall leave here!

SLAM! SLAM! SLAM! Slam! Slam! SLAM! SLAM!

ALL THE DOORS HAVE CLOSED AND LOCKED! INCLUDING THE BATHROOM!

DAMN! NOW I HAVE TO GO. AND THE CONTINUOUS DRIPPING CAUSED BY THE WALLS BLEEDING AIN'T HELPING ANY!

The first step of the ceremony is to whack yourself in the face a few times with this axe...

TIME OUT AGAIN!

And I betcha feel guilty about it, dontcha?

YEAH, ALL RIGHT, I'LL DO IT.

TIME OUT! I sort of like my soul where it is. Could I just initial a statement or something?

YOU CAN'T DO THIS ONE THING FOR ME WHEN I DIED FOR YOU?

YOU DIDN'T DIE FOR ME! I KILLED YOU!

My eternity is on trial now. I have only one hope to leave my eternal torment, and that is you. We must travel to the Court of Hell, and once they witness our love for each other, I shall be unshackled!

I can bring your soul there, but first you must perform a ceremony to remove your soul from your body.

OK. HOW DO WE GET TO THE "COURT OF HELL?"

We are journeying to eternity. what difference does it make if his mortal form dies in a Halloween costume?

TORG, DO YOU REALLY WANT TO DIE THIS WAY?

I THINK SHE WAS REFERRING TO DRIVING AN AXE INTO MY FACE MULTIPLE TIMES.

Well, if not the axe, does anyone have a nail-gun?

WE'D NEED AN EXTENSION CORD.

TORG, THERE IS SOMETHING WRONG ABOUT THIS GHOST. I DON'T SENSE LOVE TOWARDS YOU, I SENSE HATE TOWARDS SOMETHING ELSE!

GIVE IT UP, GWYNN. IT'S JUST NOT GOING TO WORK BETWEEN US.

TORG...

LOOK, WE'RE ALL GOING TO STAY TRAPPED HERE UNLESS I DO THIS, SO IT'S THE WAY IT'S GOT TO BE.

I CAN'T BELIEVE YOU'RE REALLY DOING THIS, TORG!

I NOT ONLY KILLED VAL IN THE PRESENT, BUT I DIDN'T RESCUE HER FROM HER FATE IN THE PAST WHEN I COULD HAVE. THIS IS MY LAST SHOT TO SAVE HER. I'M NOT GOING TO ABANDON HER TO HELL!

114

115

118

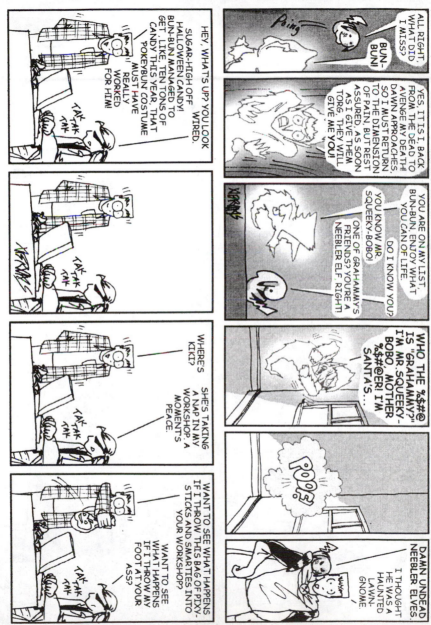

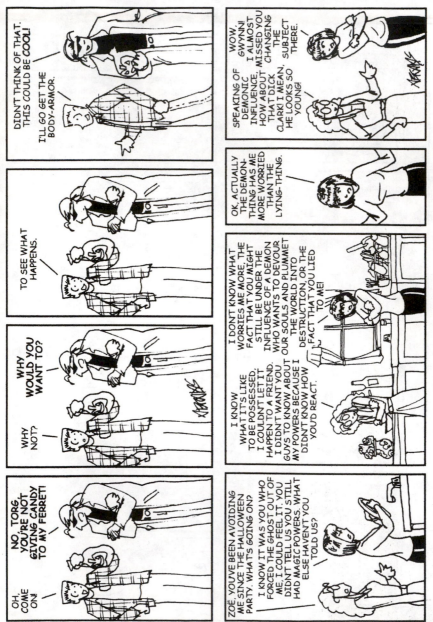

120

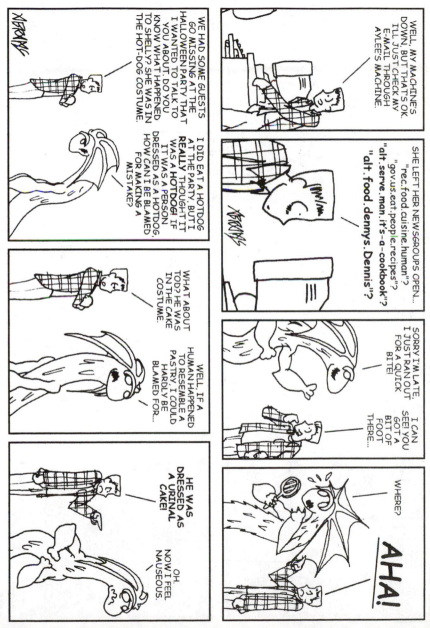

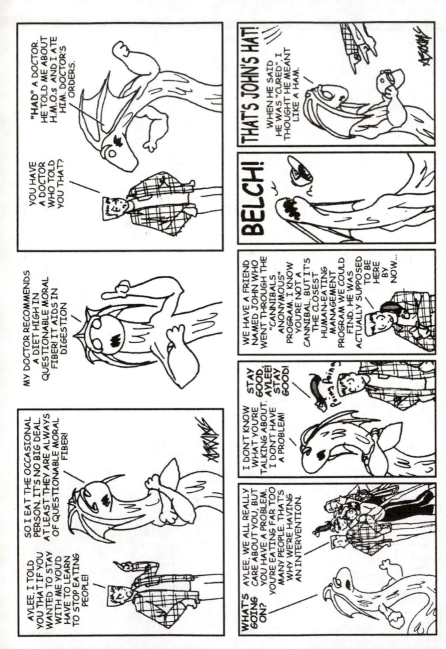

124

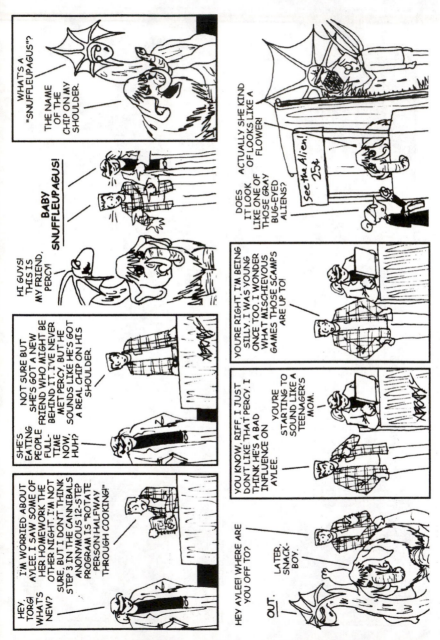

128

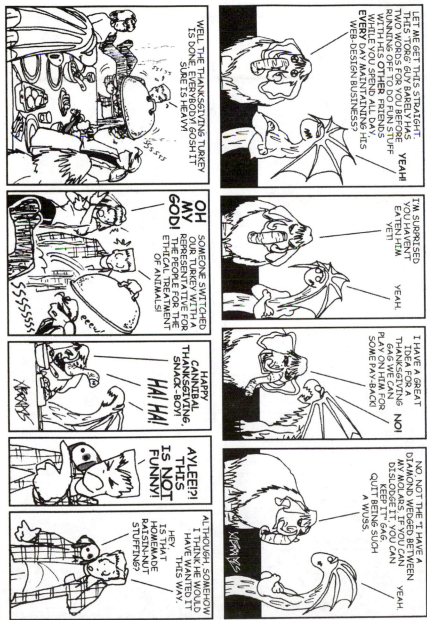

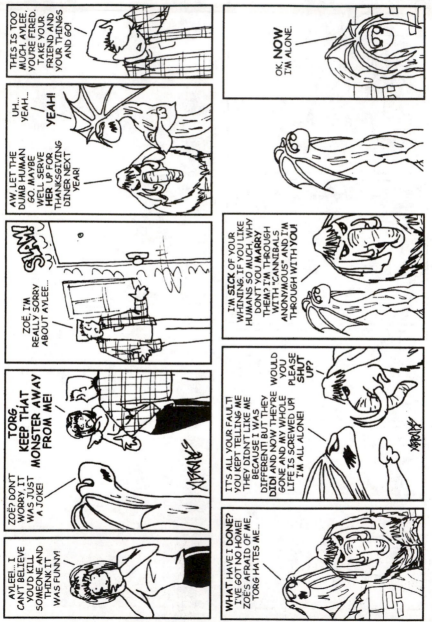

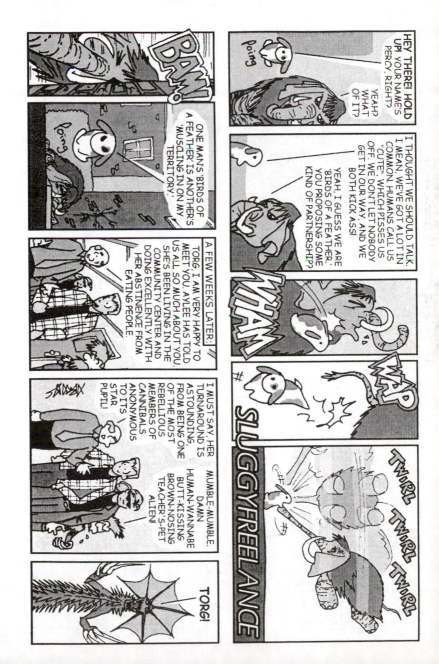

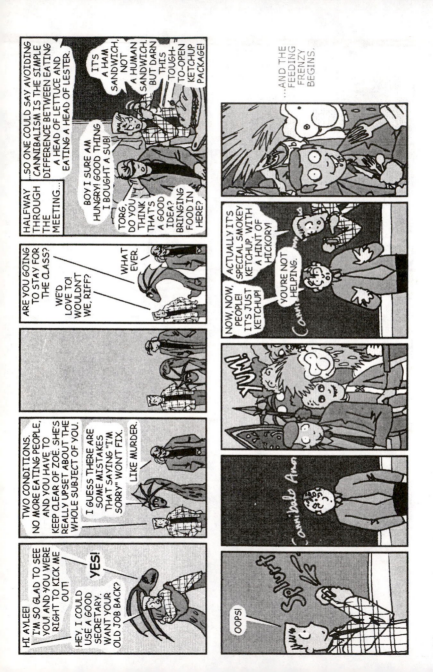

132

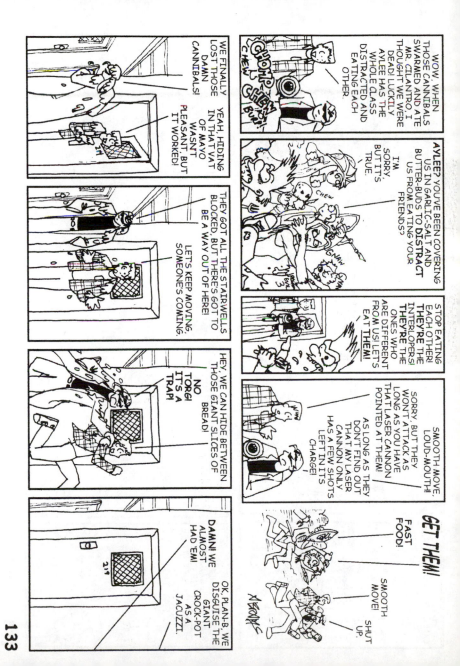

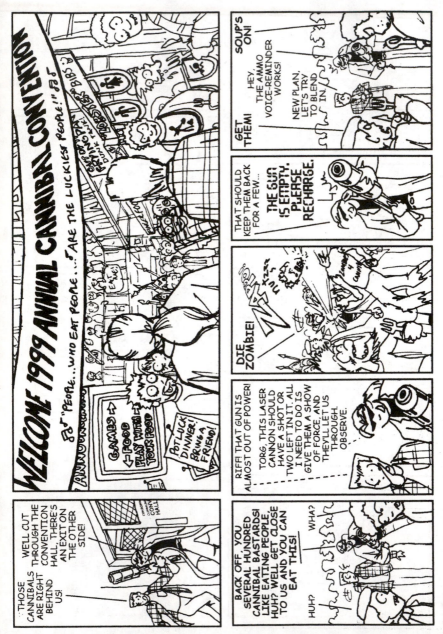

134

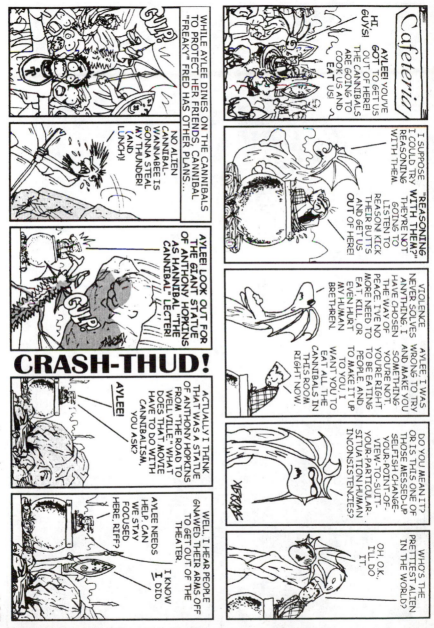

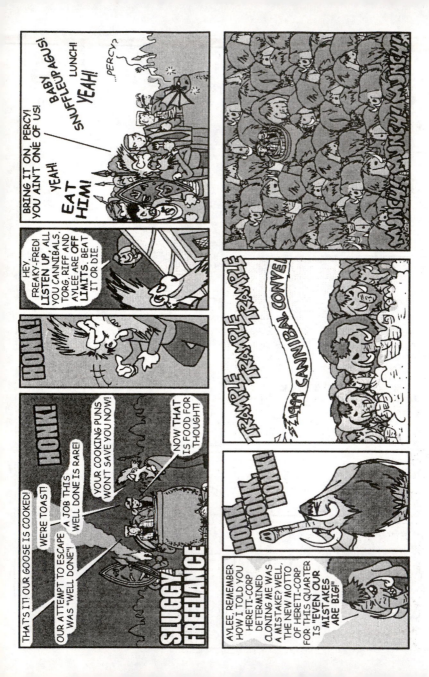

136

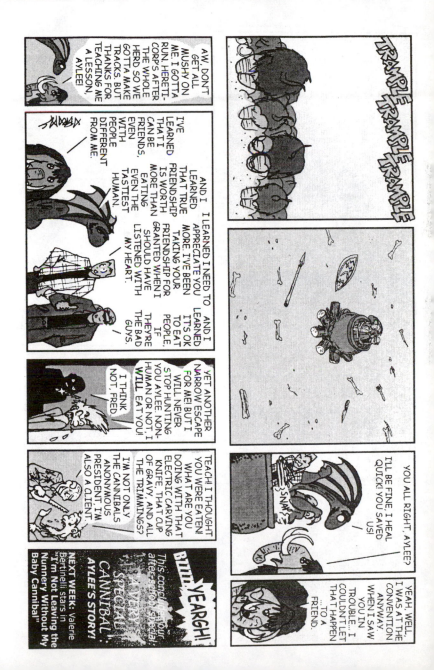

TRAMPLE TRAMPLE TRAMPLE

YOU ALL RIGHT, AYLEE?

I'LL BE FINE, I HEAL QUICK! YOU SAVED US!

SNAP!

YEAH, WELL, I WAS AT THE CONVENTION ANYWAY. WHEN I SAW YOU IN TROUBLE...I COULDN'T LET THAT HAPPEN ...TO A FRIEND.

AW, DON'T GET ALL MUSHY ON ME. I GOTTA RUN, HERE! I GOTTA MAKE TRACKS, BUT THANKS FOR TEACHING ME A LESSON, AYLEE!

I'VE LEARNED THAT TRUE FRIENDSHIP IS WORTH MORE THAN EATING FRIENDS, EVEN THE TASTIEST HUMAN.

AND I LEARNED THAT I CAN BE FRIENDS, EVEN WITH PEOPLE DIFFERENT FROM ME.

I LEARNED I NEED TO APPRECIATE YOU MORE. I'VE BEEN TAKING YOUR FRIENDSHIP FOR GRANTED WHEN I SHOULD HAVE LISTENED WITH MY HEART.

AND I LEARNED IT'S OK TO EAT PEOPLE. IF THEY'RE THE BAD GUYS.

YET ANOTHER NARROW ESCAPE FOR ME! BUT I WILL NEVER STOP HUNTING YOU AYLEE. NON-HUMAN OR NOT, I WILL EAT YOU!

I THINK NOT, FRED.

TEACH! I THOUGHT YOU WERE EATEN! WHAT ARE YOU DOING WITH THAT ELECTRIC CARVING KNIFE, THAT CUP OF GRAVY, AND ALL THE TRIMMINGS?

I'M NOT ONLY THE CANNIBALS ANONYMOUS PRESIDENT, I'M ALSO A CLIENT.

BURP! YEARGH!

This comic, in your hands, continues after this special.

AYLEE'S SPECIAL!: *CANNIBAL*: AYLEE'S STORY!

NEXT WEEK: Valerie Bertinelli stars in "I'm Not Leaving the Nunnery Without My Baby Cannibal!"

137

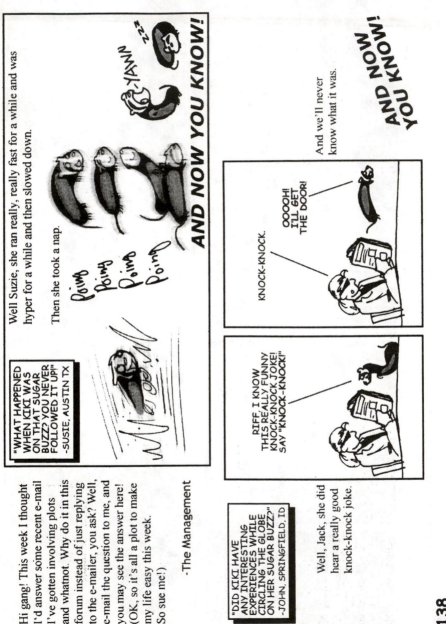

Hi gang! This week I thought I'd answer some recent e-mail I've gotten involving plots and whatnot. Why do it in this forum instead of just replying to the e-mailer, you ask? Well, e-mail the question to me, and you may see the answer here! (OK, so it's all a plot to make my life easy this week. So sue me!)

-The Management

"WHAT HAPPENED WHEN KIKI WAS ON THAT SUGAR BUZZ? YOU NEVER FOLLOWED IT UP!"
-SUSIE, AUSTIN TX

Well Suzie, she ran really, really fast for a while and was hyper for a while and then slowed down.

Then she took a nap.

-YAWN

AND NOW YOU KNOW!

"DID KIKI HAVE ANY INTERESTING EXPERIENCES WHILE CIRCLING THE GLOBE ON HER SUGAR BUZZ?"
-JOHN, SPRINGFIELD, ID

Well, Jack, she did hear a really good knock-knock joke.

RIFF, I KNOW THIS REALLY FUNNY KNOCK-KNOCK JOKE! SAY "KNOCK-KNOCK!"

KNOCK-KNOCK.

OOOOH! I'LL GET THE DOOR!

And we'll never know what it was.

AND NOW YOU KNOW!

138

"WHAT'S ZOË BEEN UP TO ALL THIS TIME? HAVEN'T SEEN/HEARD FROM HER IN A LONG TIME, IT SEEMS..."
-NANCY RENNETT

Zoë is not having a good time.

She is angry and afraid of Aylee and her habit of eating people.

She is angry and afraid of her own roommate, Gwynn, unsure of if she is controlling her demonic powers, or under their control.

She is angry and has a crush on her college classmate Dex, who "doesn't know she's alive".

And she is overall sad. Her grades are down and she's almost out of money.

"WHAT ABOUT GWYNN'S MAGIC POWERS? YOU KIND OF FORGOT ABOUT GWYNN'S MAGIC POWERS DURING THE WHOLE CANNIBALISM THING... ARE GWYNN'S MAGIC POWERS STILL GOING TO BE AN ISSUE?"
-REV. VICTOR W. PROUD INVENTOR OF THE WHEEL.

Gwynn has become a classic Shakespearean tragic hero, walking a line between embracing her power, hiding from it, and getting Laser Eye Surgery.

GOOD

BAD

KRK

GLASSES-FREE

But she's looking forward to her Holiday Break and at least this week she's dressed as Oasis!

I'M NOT COMING OUT DRESSED LIKE THIS!

AND NOW YOU KNOW!

Now I'm overall sad.

Before you try to guess which path she will take, remember the problems laser eye surgery caused Hamlet. I can say no more, for I have already said too much.

All right, I'll say this much, dating Riff appears to have turned her off to the laser eye surgery for now.

ZAP ZAP ZAP **AND NOW YOU KNOW!**

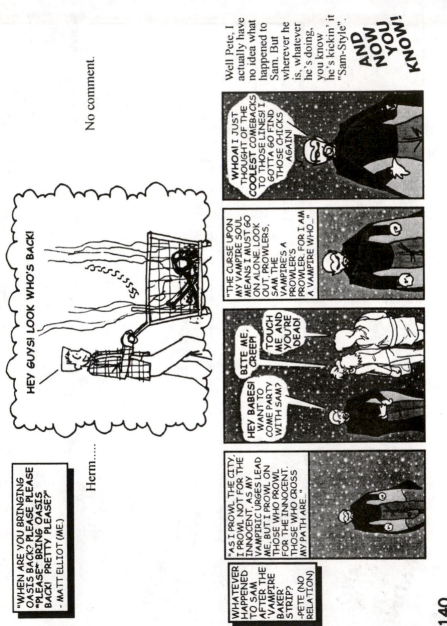

"WHEN ARE YOU BRINGING OASIS BACK? PLEASE PLEASE "PLEASE~ BRING OASIS BACK! PRETTY PLEASE?"
- MATT ELLIOT (ME.)

Herm.....

No comment.

WHATEVER HAPPENED TO SAM AFTER THE 'VAMPIRE BAKER' STRIP?
-PETE (NO RELATION)

Well Pete, I actually have no idea what happened to Sam. But wherever he is, whatever he's doing, you know he's kickin' it "Sam-Style".

AND NOW YOU KNOW!

140

"HEY, CAN WE HAVE MORE STICK-FIGURES IN YOUR COMIC? AND HOW ABOUT SOME STICK-FIGURE MERCHANDISE?"
-TOM, SHIRT-GUY

How convenient and spontaneous of you to ask, Shirt-guy Tom! And what a great way to wrap up **SLUGGY FREELANCE ANSWERS YOUR E-MAIL VACATION WEEK!**

Look what I got for you all today!:

THE OFFICIAL SLUGGY FREELANCE STICK-FIGURE TRADING CARDS!

Just print, clip, snip, and split your lip!
Trade with your friends!
A new set every day!*
Don't miss this one day event!

*Offer void if yesterday is not today.

AND NOW YOU KNOW**!

(**Now you know how lame a vacation week can be!)

Zoë

Torg

Riff

141

142

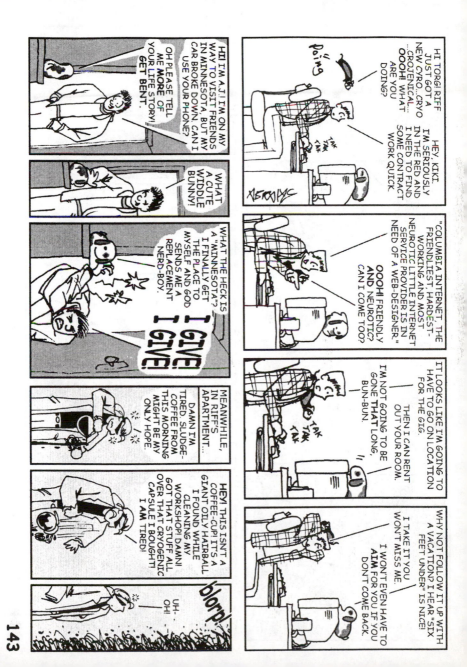

143

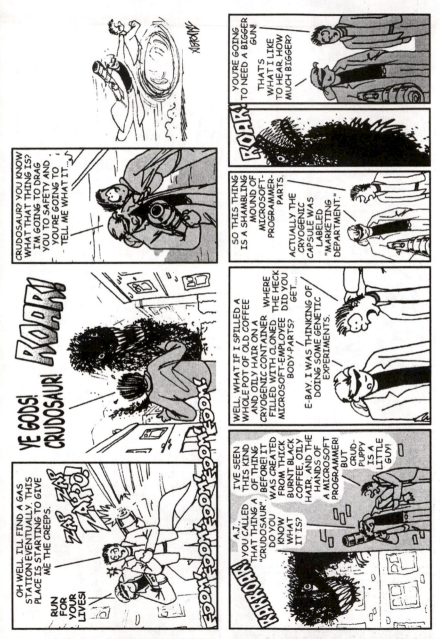

144

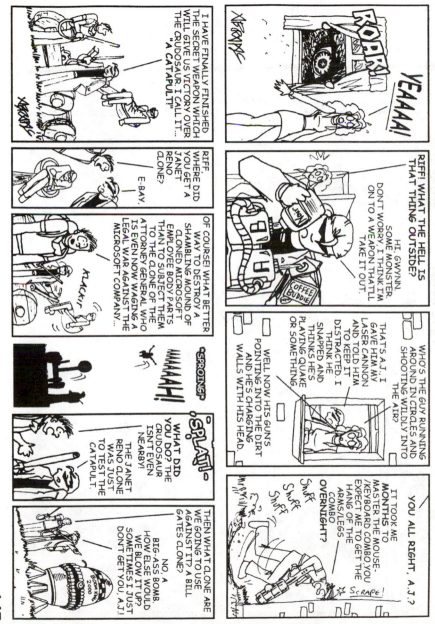

YEAAA!!

I HAVE FINALLY FINISHED THE SECRET WEAPON WHICH WILL GIVE US VICTORY OVER THE CRUDOSAUR. I CALL IT... "A CATAPULT."

RIFF! WHERE DID YOU GET A JANET RENO CLONE?

E-BAY.

OF COURSE! WHAT BETTER WAY TO DESTROY A SHAMBLING MOUND OF CLONED MICROSOFT EMPLOYEE BODY PARTS THAN TO SUBJECT THEM TO THE CLONE OF THE ATTORNEY GENERAL WHO IS EVEN NOW WAGING A LEGAL WAR AGAINST THE MICROSOFT COMPANY...

KLACKIT!

"SPROING!"

WHAAAH!!

RIFF! WHAT THE HELL IS THAT THING OUTSIDE?

HI, GWYNN. SOME MONSTER. DON'T WORRY, I THINK I'M ON TO A WEAPON THAT'LL TAKE IT OUT.

WHO'S THE GUY RUNNING AROUND IN CIRCLES AND SHOOTING WILDLY INTO THE AIR?

THAT'S A.J. I GAVE HIM MY LASER CANNON AND TOLD HIM TO KEEP IT TO KEEP IT DISTRACTED. I THINK HE SNAPPED AND THINKS HE'S PLAYING QUAKE OR SOMETHING.

WELL NOW HIS GUN'S POINTING INTO THE DIRT AND HE'S CHARGING WALLS WITH HIS HEAD.

YOU ALL RIGHT, A.J.?

IT TOOK ME MONTHS TO MASTER THE MOUSE-/KEYBOARD COMBO.YOU EXPECT ME TO GET THE HANG OF THE ARMS/LEGS COMBO **OVERNIGHT**?

Shuff Shuff Shuff

SCRAPE!

"SPLAT!"

WHAT DID YOU DO? THE CRUDOSAUR ISN'T EVEN NEARBY!

THE JANET RENO CLONE WAS JUST TO TEST THE CATAPULT.

THEN WHAT CLONE ARE WE GOING TO USE AGAINST IT? A BILL GATES CLONE?

NO. A BIG-ASS BOMB. HOW ELSE WOULD WE BLOW IT UP? SOMETIMES I JUST DON'T GET YOU, A.J.!

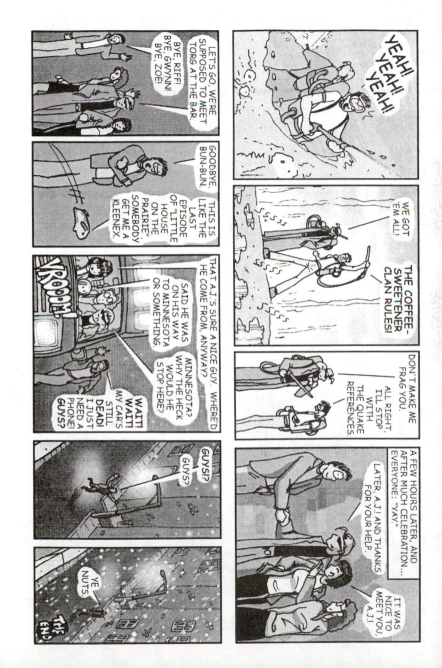

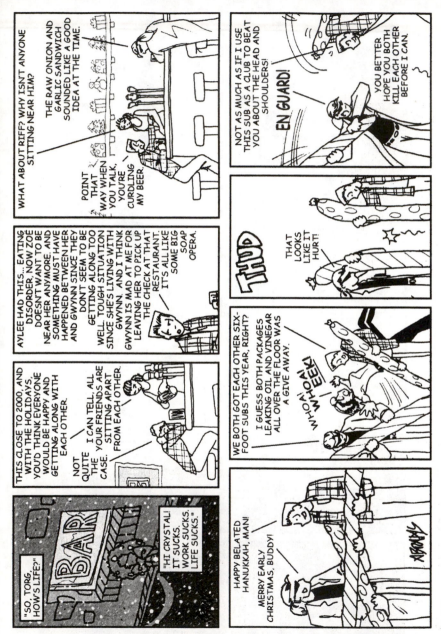

148

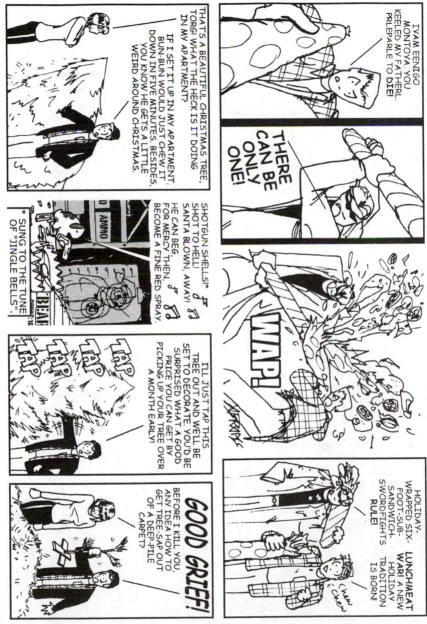

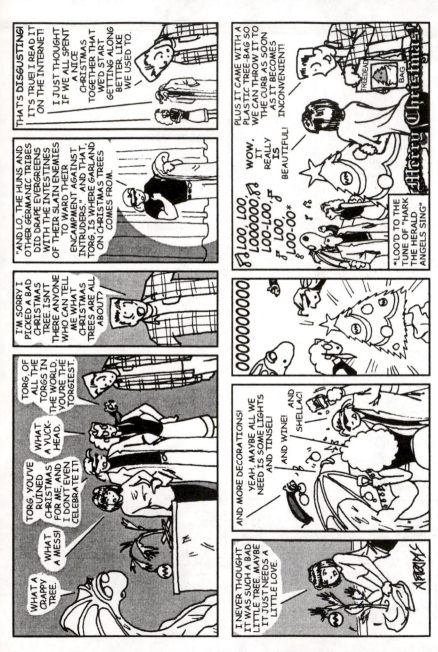

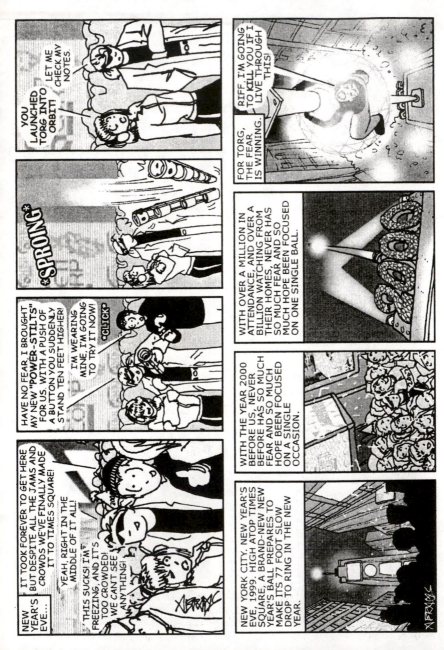

154

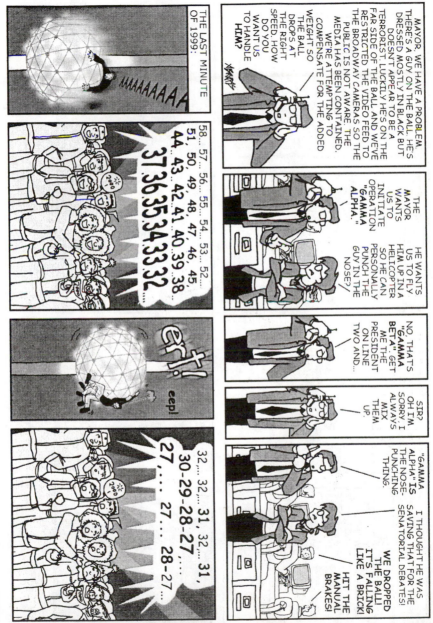

GOOD NEWS, MAYOR! WE ADJUSTED THE VIDEO-FEED SPEED SO THE FOLKS AT HOME WILL NEVER KNOW THE BALL MALFUNCTIONED! AND WHAT'S EVEN BETTER, THE GUY ON THE BALL FELL OFF! SO THE LAST TEN SECONDS OF THE COUNTDOWN WILL GO FLAWLESSLY!

UM... NO SIR, I DON'T KNOW WHERE THE GUY FELL. NO REPORTS OF A "JUMPER". IT DOESN'T MATTER, WE MADE IT! WE'RE DOWN TO THE LAST 10 SECONDS!

"5"

"6"

"7"

"8"

156

HAPPY YEAR 200!

200

Ok, so technically it's 2000, but it says 200! In any case, welcome to the New Millennium!

OK, so technically it's not the new millennium until 2001, but it sure feels "millennium-ish"!

Wishing you and yours a happy Millennium-Ish-Thingy-2000!

safe and
hurray!
hic

Cheers!

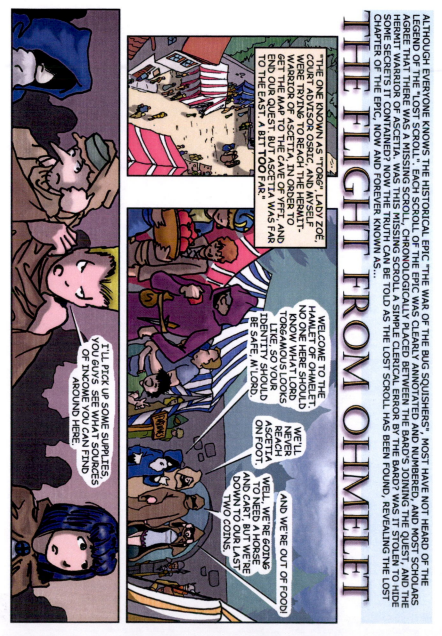

THE FLIGHT FROM OHMELET

ALTHOUGH EVERYONE KNOWS THE HISTORICAL EPIC "THE WAR OF THE BUG SQUISHERS", MOST HAVE NOT HEARD OF THE LEGEND OF THE "LOST SCROLL". EACH SCROLL OF THE EPIC WAS CLEARLY ANNOTATED AND NUMBERED, AND MOST SCHOLARS AGREE THAT THERE WAS A MISSING SCROLL, CHRONOLOGICALLY PLACED BETWEEN THE BARD'S JOINING THE QUEST, AND THE HERMIT WARRIOR OF ASCETIA. WAS THIS MISSING SCROLL A SIMPLE CLERICAL ERROR BY THE BARD? WAS IT STOLEN TO HIDE SOME SECRETS IT CONTAINED? NOW THE TRUTH CAN BE TOLD AS THE LOST SCROLL HAS BEEN FOUND, REVEALING THE LOST CHAPTER OF THE EPIC, NOW AND FOREVER KNOWN AS...

"THE ONE KNOWN AS "TORG" LADY ZOË, COURT ADVISOR OSRIC, AND MYSELF WERE TRYING TO REACH THE HERMIT-WARRIOR OF ASCETIA, IN ORDER TO GET THE MAP TO THE CAVE OF YFFI, AND END OUR QUEST. BUT ASCETIA WAS FAR TO THE EAST. A BIT TOO FAR."

WELCOME TO THE HAMLET OF OHMELET. NO ONE HERE SHOULD KNOW WHAT LORD TORGAMOUS LOOKS LIKE, SO YOUR IDENTITY SHOULD BE SAFE, M'LORD.

WE'LL NEVER REACH ASCETIA ON FOOT.

AND WE'RE OUT OF FOOD!

WELL, WE'RE GOING TO NEED A HORSE AND CART, BUT WE'RE DOWN TO OUR LAST TWO COINS.

I'LL PICK UP SOME SUPPLIES, YOU GUYS SEE WHAT SOURCES OF INCOME YOU CAN FIND AROUND HERE.

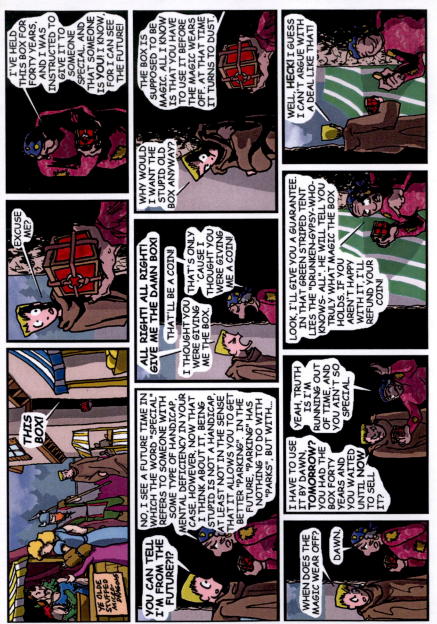

160

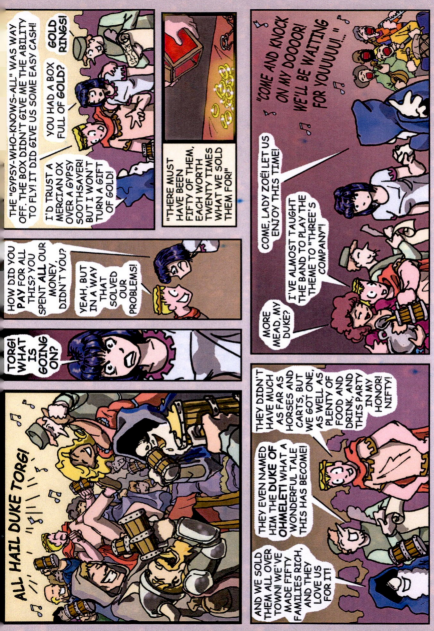

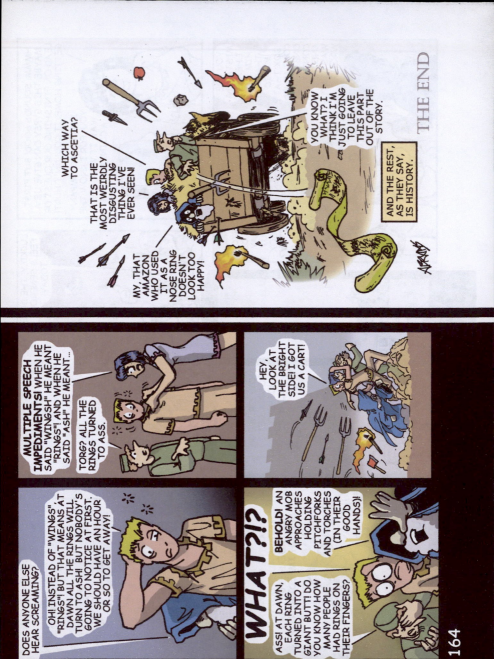